for James, Rebecca and Sally Maidment

Unicorn is a registered trademark of E. P. Dutton.
Library of Congress number 86-198950
ISBN 0-525-44608-7
First published in the United States 1986 by
Dutton Children's Books,
a division of Penguin Books USA Inc.
Originally published in England 1986 by
Andersen Press Limited
62-65 Chandos Place, London WC2N 4NW
Printed in Hong Kong by South China Printing Co.
First Unicorn Edition 1990
10 9 8 7 6 5 4 3 2 1

Our Cat Flossie

RUTH BROWN

DUTTON CHILDREN'S BOOKS · NEW YORK

This is our cat Flossie.

She lives with us in the city.

She likes the house and the garden, but does not
get on very well with the neighbors.

Her hobbies include bird watching

and fishing.

Flossie is a skillful climber

and an enthusiastic gardener.

She always insists on helping with knitting

and making the beds.

She is very good at polishing shoes

but not quite so useful at Christmastime.

There are two things that she hates—
the sound of fireworks

and visits to the vet.

Flossie loves collecting butterflies,

and she is rather fond of snails,

even though she finds them puzzling.

She is unable to resist a box

no matter what the size.

But like all cats, mostly she loves to sleep...

and sleep...

and sleep.